THE ORPHAN AND THE POLAR BEAR

Published by Inhabit Media Inc.
www.inhabitmedia.com

Edited by: Louise Flaherty and Neil Christopher
Written by: Sakiasi Qaunaq
Translated by: Rachel A. Qitsualik
Art Direction by: Neil Christopher
Illustrations by: Eva Widermann

Inhabit Media Inc.

Nunavut: P.O. Box 11125, Iqaluit, Nunavut, X0A 1H0
Ontario: 146A Orchard View Blvd., Toronto, Ontario, M4R 1C3

We acknowledge the support of the Canada Council for the Arts for our publishing program.

Canada Council Conseil des Arts
for the Arts   du Canada

Printed by MCRL Overseas Printing Inc. in ShenZhen, China.
August 2011 Job # 4236067-3

ISBN 978-1-926569-44-4

Library and Archives Canada Cataloguing in Publication

Qaunaq, Sakiasi, 1942-
The orphan and the polar bear / retold by Sakiasi
Qaunaq ; illustrated by Eva Widermann.

(Unikkaakuluit series)
ISBN 978-1-926569-44-4

1. Inuit--Juvenile fiction. 2. Inuit mythology.
3. Inuit--Folklore. I. Widermann, Eva II. Title.
III. Series: Unikkaakuluit series

PS8633.A96O77 2011 jC813'.6 C2011-904243-6

THE ORPHAN AND THE POLAR BEAR

RETOLD BY

SAKIASI QAUNAQ

ILLUSTRATED BY

EVA WIDERMANN

FOREWORD

Both of us grew up listening to traditional stories. These tales captured our imaginations with their heroes, monsters, adventures, and humour. We believe that folktales, myths, and legends are an important part of culture and identity, and we have been working with the Qikiqtani Inuit Association and the Nunavut Government to ensure that these important stories are preserved and made available to future generations of Nunavummiut.

Over the last few years, we have been partnering with Nunavummiut storytellers and writers to create books inspired by the rich storytelling traditions of Inuit. When we heard Sakiasi Qaunaq's version of *The Orphan and the Polar Bear,* we immediately knew that this story needed to be made into a children's book.

Many traditional themes and values are represented in this legend. As you read this story, imagine your ancestors telling stories like these. Think about what these tales might have meant to the people listening.

We hope that you enjoy this story and that you will continue to explore the rich storytelling tradition of the Canadian North.

Louise Flaherty and Neil Christopher
Inhabit Media Inc.

Long ago, when people didn't have rifles, they hunted walrus using harpoons. The winter hunts took place at the floe edge, where there is open water and moving ice.

In the land where this story takes place, there lived a people who hunted in this traditional manner.

A little orphan from the camp often accompanied the men on these hunts. This orphan had lost his father and mother and lived with his grandmother.

At the end of each hunt, the men would return home without the orphan. They would abandon him at the floe edge. Each time the men left him, the little boy had to walk all the way back to camp. This was a very long walk and it would be night by the time he arrived.

Every time the men went hunting, the orphan boy would be ordered to go along with them. And, every time, he would be abandoned at the end of the hunt!

After being left behind at the end of yet another hunt, the boy began following the tracks of the dog teams to find his way home. Hearing the sound of someone walking behind him, he spun around to find himself face to face with a huge polar bear. The boy assumed a hunter's stance, flung his harpoon, and missed. Then the bear transformed into a large man—he was an older man, but powerful looking—and spoke to the boy.

"I have seen how the adults mistreat you, and I have often felt great pity for your situation. I wish to teach you the skills you need to survive, so that you will no longer be dependant on these cruel people. Climb on my back and come with me to my village."

Then the man transformed back into a polar bear and invited the orphan to ride on his back. After the little orphan was safely seated on the back of the bear, they left and travelled far, far away.

They travelled a great distance into the open sea and finally came to an island inhabited by a community of polar bears. The bear that had befriended the little orphan was an elder, and the leader of this camp of bears.

While living in
the camp, the
boy undertook
training to
become a
capable hunter.

He was given his
own harpoon,
complete with a
sharp sakku (harpoon
head). He went along on seal
hunts at aglus (seal breathing holes). On many of these hunts, fortune was with
the little orphan and he would often manage to harpoon a seal.

During one such hunt, a large bear came loping up to the boy. He pushed the orphan aside and stole his catch. Once again, the little orphan was being mistreated. This became a common occurrence during the hunts, so the orphan went to speak to the bear elder who had brought him to the camp.

After telling the story of how the other bear would deprive him of his catch, the orphan was given the following advice:

"Next time, wait while the bear runs up behind you. When he has almost reached you, turn quickly and stab him with your harpoon."

17

The next day when they went out for a hunt, the same large bear waited until the orphan caught a seal. Then the bear charged toward the boy, intending to steal his catch. To the bear's surprise, the orphan turned just in time to harpoon him. The orphan's aim was good, and the bear collapsed onto the ice. The orphan's tormentor lay dead on the ice and the body was left behind when they all went home.

That night, the entire polar bear camp heard the sounds of the big bear's arrival. The bear that they had left dead on the ice had returned to the camp. The big bear shouted:

"Little orphan, come out!"

"Don't do it, don't do it," the orphan was told by the polar bear elder.

"Little orphan, come out!"

"Don't do it, don't do it. Don't go out," the elder bear said again.

The angry voice boomed again, "Little orphan, come out!"

"All right, go out now," said the elder bear.

And so the orphan went out to meet the bear he had harpooned. As he approached, the orphan was surprised to see a smile on the bear's face. He held the orphan's harpoon head in his paw and extended his reach to return it to its owner.

Although the orphan went hunting many times with the polar bears, the big bear who had stolen his catch so many times before never bothered him again. From that day onward, the boy was always very well treated during the hunts. When the orphan would tell the bears about how humans had mistreated him, the big bear would say, "I wish I could find some people to push down. They look so silly standing on their skinny legs."

To this the bear elder would reply, "Never talk that way! The humans use our cousins, the dogs, to protect their camps and hunt us. Our cousins can be very dangerous to us, so don't make the humans our enemy. Stay clear of them and their camps."

The wise elder bear was full of knowledge about the world. He taught the other bears many lessons about how to survive on the land, just as he had taught the little orphan.

After participating in many hunts, the orphan finally gained the skills and knowledge necessary to manage on his own. He had learned all that he could from the elder bear.

One day, instead of taking the orphan out on another hunt, the elder bear began the long journey back to the human world across the sea. When they finally reached the place where they had first met, the bear elder left the orphan. Then the boy began the long walk back toward his village.

And that is the story of how a boy was trained by polar bears to become a man and a capable hunter.

About the Author

Sakiasi Qaunaq was born in 1942, at Alangnarjuk, a campsite near Igloolik, but has lived most of his life in the Arctic Bay area. His grandmother told him stories as a child—including *The Orphan and the Polar Bear*—and fostered in him a love for traditional legends that persists to this day. In his youth the stories were told for entertainment, but today he feels their retelling is crucial to the sustaining of Inuit traditions and culture.